I ESCAPED THE TOWER OF LONDON

ELLIE CROWE

SCOTT PETERS

I Escaped The Tower of London (I Escaped Book Eight)

Copyright © 2021 by Ellie Crowe & Scott Peters

Library of Congress Control Number:

ISBN: (Hardcover)

ISBN: 978-1-951019-24-2 (Paperback)

Book cover design by Susan Wyshynski

Best Day Books For Young Readers

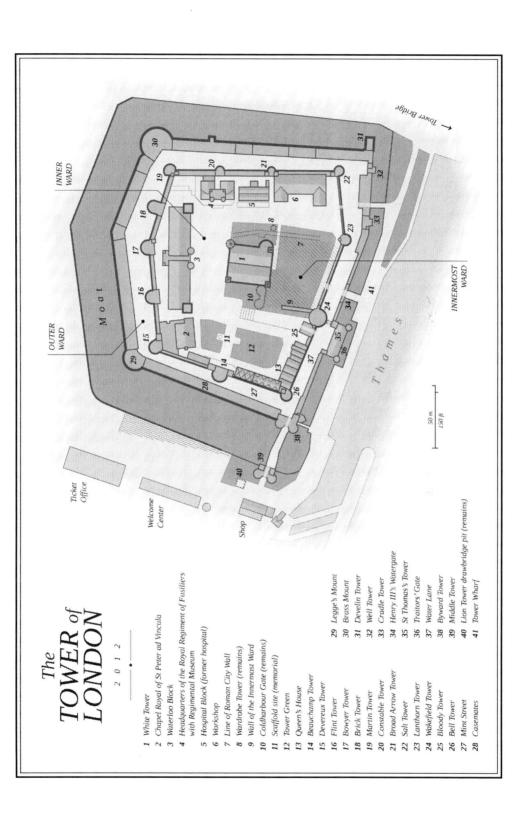

The TOWER of LONDON

2012

1 White Tower
2 Chapel Royal of St Peter ad Vincula
3 Waterloo Block
4 Headquarters of the Royal Regiment of Fusiliers
  with Regimental Museum
5 Hospital Block (former hospital)
6 Workshop
7 Line of Roman City Wall
8 Wardrobe Tower (remains)
9 Wall of the Innermost Ward
10 Coldharbour Gate (remains)
11 Scaffold site (memorial)
12 Tower Green
13 Queen's House
14 Beauchamp Tower
15 Devereux Tower
16 Flint Tower
17 Bowyer Tower
18 Brick Tower
19 Martin Tower
20 Constable Tower
21 Broad Arrow Tower
22 Salt Tower
23 Lanthorn Tower
24 Wakefield Tower
25 Bloody Tower
26 Bell Tower
27 Mint Street
28 Casemates
29 Legge's Mount
30 Brass Mount
31 Develin Tower
32 Well Tower
33 Cradle Tower
34 Henry III's Watergate
35 St Thomas's Tower
36 Traitors' Gate
37 Water Lane
38 Byward Tower
39 Middle Tower
40 Lion Tower drawbridge pit (remains)
41 Tower Wharf

INNER WARD

OUTER WARD

INNERMOST WARD

Moat

Thames

Tower Bridge

Ticket Office

Welcome Center

Shop

50 m
150 ft

CHAPTER ONE

The Tower of London
The Dungeon Among the Rats
Year 1554

Fifteen-year-old Ben opened his eyes.

All he could see was black.

Pitch-black.

Where was he?

A dungeon?

Under his cheek, the damp earth floor smelled musty. His hands, arms, wrists, and jaw throbbed. Groaning, Ben struggled to his feet. His head smashed into the ceiling. With a shout, he lost his balance and stumbled, but something had hold of his ankle. As he fell, a metallic rattle jangled near his foot.

Zooks! What now?

Ben reached for his leg. Someone had clamped a

metal cuff above his foot—they'd chained him to the floor! Frantic, he tried to pull loose.

Ouch.

Metal sliced into his skin, and warm blood oozed. He touched it and raised his fingers to his eyes.

It was terrifyingly dark. Too dark to see.

Yes. This *had* to be a dungeon. He knew exactly where he'd been locked up.

In the Tower of London.

He was a prisoner, and he'd never escape.

Getting to his feet, more carefully this time, he explored as far as the chain would allow. He ran his hands over the earthen walls, trying to find a loose rock to smash the chain open.

Nothing.

The dungeon's furthest corner reeked of pee. He wrinkled his nose and backed away. The toilet. Great.

Time passed. The silence grew deafening. Where were the guards? Even seeing a guard would be better than seeing no one. Had they left him to die alone? He longed to hear a voice. Maybe another prisoner nearby?

"Is anyone here?" Ben called.

Silence.

Ben began to shiver as the cold seeped into his bones. Hunger twisted his stomach. He couldn't remember the last time he'd eaten. Or even had a sip of water. His teeth chattered.

Think, he told himself. *Don't give way to panic. Don't give up. Never ever give up. Think.*

To his astonishment, an odd trickling sound began along the left wall. It sounded like . . . water? Yes, like dripping water. Confused, Ben moved toward it. Soft wetness splashed underfoot. The cell floor was growing muddy and soon his boots were soaked. The water was rising.

Ben knew the dungeon sat alongside the River Thames. Sometimes, the water rose over the river's banks and flooded the Tower.

An awful thought struck. Were they going to drown him down here?

"Help!" Ben shouted. "Help!"

No answer.

Something rustled in the far corner. His ears pricked.

"Who's there?"

More rustling.

"Who's there? Tell me who you are!" He clenched his fists, ready to defend himself.

Tiny teeth bit his ankle.

"Hey!" he shouted, kicking out.

Scurrying, chittering sounds filled the dungeon. Tiny click-click-clicks. Like claws scratching across stone.

Rats! It had to be rats. Another sharp bite. In horror, he knew this awful place. Once, when Ben was making his daily rounds delivering the Tower's coal, the Tower Guards had whispered about it.

The Dungeon Among the Rats.

During high tide, the moat overflowed, pouring into the cell. When it did, rats swam into the dungeon.

It was rat-time, and he was here alone.

He squinted into the dark depths, his muscles tense. Rats were carnivorous and ate human flesh. In the poor street where he lived, women dared not leave their babies alone. Rats sensed the sick, or the small, or the helpless. And here he was chained up, with a bleeding ankle.

He pictured the rats squeaking, "Ooh, a person. All chained up and can't get away. Bleeding, too! Let's have a nice little rat-feast."

Ben shuddered and kicked left and right with his un-chained leg.

He wished he'd never brought his coal cart anywhere near the Tower of London. He wished he'd never walked through the Tower's spooky gates. If he'd stayed away, he'd never have been thrown into the scariest place in all of England.

He had to get out. He had to survive.

He had to escape!

CHAPTER TWO

RIVER THAMES
THE TOWER OF LONDON
ONE WEEK EARLIER

"Help! Help me!" The girl's voice was shrill and terrified.

Her scream came from the direction of the Traitors' Gate. The dark, moss-covered entrance along the River Thames led to England's ominous Tower of London.

Ben grabbed his fishing pole, the only available weapon, and ran toward the frightened cries.

His best friend, Tim, sprinting as fast as he could on bowlegs, raced after him. "Stop, you nincompoop. Look at all those armed guards!"

"Zooks." Ben skidded to a halt. "Something strange is going on. They're taking a female prisoner to the Tower."

"Who is she?" Tim said. "Looks like someone important."

The girl cried out again. "I will not go through the Traitor's Gate. I am not a traitor!"

Fishermen craned to see what was happening. Pedestrians on London Bridge leaned over to check out the commotion.

Ben studied the official-looking barge docked at the Traitor's Gate. The terrified girl on deck looked only a few years older than himself. She wore a beautiful white cape with a black fur collar. Her gloved hands clung to the rails. Nobles in fur cloaks and uniformed guards surrounded her.

"Will not one of you help me?" the girl called to the watching crowd.

Ben bit his lip. Why on earth would they lock up a girl like that in the Tower of London?

Wind whipped her cloak. The River Thames sloshed as waves crashed against the barge. Thunder boomed, and the dark sky sent a sudden bucket of icy rain pouring down, drenching her red ringlets.

Ben pulled his shirt collar higher. "Who is she?" he asked a fisherman. "What are they doing to her?"

"It's Princess Elizabeth," the gray-bearded man muttered.

Princess Elizabeth?

Ben couldn't help a small gasp.

The fisherman shook his head angrily. "They're locking the Princess up in the Tower."

A woman chimed in, clicking her tongue. "And through the Traitor's Gate, too—like she's a traitor. What's she done? Nothing."

The fisherman clenched his fists. "Her mother, Queen Anne Boleyn, was taken through the Traitor's Gate. A few weeks later, they chopped off her head."

Ben gaped. "Surely they won't execute the Princess?"

"Only the doomed are brought through the Traitor's Gate," the fisherman said, blinking in the rain.

"This is horrible. My ma and pa, when they were alive, they loved the Princess."

"Aye, most do," the fisherman said.

"England's Hope, that's what Ma and Pa called her. And now she's to be executed?"

"Not much hope now for England's future," the fisherman said. "Not with Bloody Mary on the throne."

"She must be scared out of her wits." Ben pushed toward the barge.

Tim caught up and pulled on Ben's arm. "It's none of your concern, stay out of it, Ben."

A woman shouted, "God save you, your Grace."

A man shouted, "God save you from Bloody Mary!"

Another shouted, "God save us all from Bloody Mary. She'll destroy England."

These people hate Queen Mary, Ben thought. I do too. If not for her cruel laws, my parents would still be alive.

Tower Guards began to pull the Princess from the boat.

"I am not a traitor!" Princess Elizabeth cried.

Ben moved closer, with Tim on his heels. The massive Traitors' Gate opened on creaking hinges. Six armed sentries holding flaming torches stomped out from under the Tower's arch. They marched down the moss-covered steps. The Tower Lieutenant followed, along with yeoman warders dressed in red and blue uniforms and black hats.

Why so many guards? What did they expect would happen?

"Look at those muskets!" Tim shoved a ginger curl out of his eyes with a coal-stained hand. "Do they need all that to imprison one girl?"

"Not a girl, a princess. She's England's hope for peace. They must think someone's going to try to help her escape," Ben said.

"That would be madness."

Ben said nothing.

He wished someone would stand up and fight. He wished the people would rise up and rebel.

How could they lock up an innocent girl in the Tower of London?

CHAPTER THREE

The crowd stood breathless, waiting to see what would happen next. The Tower Lieutenant tried to help Princess Elizabeth down from the barge. She wouldn't budge.

"I am the daughter of King Henry VIII," she shouted, frantically surveying the crowd. "Will no one help me?"

Her terrified glance landed on Ben. Her golden-brown eyes were wide, framed with dark lashes. Ben wanted to run forward, but what could he do?

"Please," she called to him in a trembling voice. "Help me!"

Ben tried to think. Could he get the crowd to rise up? Could they save her? If only he had a horse. A fast horse. He could ride in, pull the Princess up onto his saddle, and be off—before those fat yeoman warders with their frilled collars and black hats could stop him.

But he had no horse.

Ben sagged with an awful feeling of guilt. Cold rain soaked his dark hair and drizzled into the collar of his threadbare, brown woolen coat.

The Tower Lieutenant claimed the Princess's attention. "Come or be carried. You must come inside, I dare not disobey Queen Mary's commands."

"Queen Mary's commands," Ben muttered. "He's just like the soldiers who murdered my ma and pa."

Tim said, "Shh, keep your voice down!"

The Princess sat down defiantly. "I will not go in there. I would rather leap into the River Thames!"

"She's brave," Ben said.

"Aye." The gray-bearded fisherman nodded. "Not much good that will do her. Her mother, Queen Anne Boleyn, was brave too. And beautiful. Before old King Henry-the-Eighth had her executed."

"No wonder the Princess is scared," Ben growled, his hands fisting.

Tim's freckled face scrunched in sympathy. "No one ever escapes the Tower of London."

A fisherwoman said, "It's bad when your own sister hates you." Her chapped hands pulled her woolen shawl tighter around her shoulders. "But worse when your sister is Bloody Queen Mary."

"Hold your tongue," the fisherman muttered. "You don't want the guards hearing."

"You'd think Queen Mary would be nicer," the fisherwoman whispered. "The Princess is an orphan. Her half-sister is all she has."

Ben swallowed hard. It was awful to be an orphan, to lose the ones you loved best, the ones who loved you. Bloody Mary's guards had killed Ma and Pa last year when he was fourteen. And for nothing!

Thunder rolled. Rain poured down.

"You'd better come in, Madame," the Lieutenant of the Tower said. "You'll grow ill sitting here in this downpour."

"Better here than in a worse place." She found Ben's eyes again. In almost a whisper, she croaked out, "Will no one help me?"

Instinctively, he moved toward her.

Three guards snapped their weapons into position and trained them on Ben. Tim hauled Ben backward.

Lightning zig-zagged across the sky, lighting the Tower's many turrets.

"Enough." The Lieutenant motioned to a pair of burly Beefeaters dressed in crimson cloaks. They took hold of the Princess under her arms, hauled her to standing, and half-carried her under the arch. With a last glance over her shoulder, the Princess was gone.

The crowd fell into a stunned silence.

It's over, Ben thought. Who was he to think he could have helped?

"Of all the buildings inside, I hope they don't imprison her in what they call the Bloody Tower," the fisherman's wife whispered. "Like the two young princes who were never seen again."

Tim found his tongue. "They're dead. Their ghosts haunt the halls. Warder John told me he saw them, wandering and moaning."

"Sounds like you know a lot about the place," the fisherman said.

Tim nodded. "Me and Ben, we work for the coalman. We deliver coal to the Tower. Some rich prisoners get to have fires."

Ben said, "I don't much like going in there." He studied the familiar towers, ramparts, and fortifications. According to Pa, the Norman warrior king, William the Conqueror, had built the massive fortress to show all of England that he was in charge. "A lot of bad stuff has happened in the Tower."

"Zooks!" Tim gasped. "I thought of something awful. What if the Princess sees her mother's ghost? Just yesterday, a guard told me he saw her, all misty, with her long cloak trailing behind her. She had no head."

"No head, poor thing!" the fisherman's wife cried.

Tim said. "Then he saw she was carrying it, holding her chopped-off head under her right arm. He nearly fainted from fright."

Ben groaned, spooked by the thought of the Princess seeing her own mother's ghost. Trust Tim to come up with something like that.

"Maybe there'll be a way for her to escape," he blurted.

"You would say that," Tim said. "You're crazy, my friend. How could she escape?"

Together they stared at the fortress. Ben pictured the spiral stone stairwells where he climbed up and down with buckets of coal. The place was a maze of cold, creepy towers, all protected by a thick wall and moat. As for the dungeons, they looked ready to swallow you up.

"Wait," Tim said. "Next time we're in there, you better not try and help her, you hare-brained nincompoop."

"I wouldn't. That would be stupid." He lowered his voice. "I wish I could, though. Ma and Pa said Princess Elizabeth should be queen. They said she'd make England peaceful and safe. Instead, Bloody Mary is queen, and she's burning Protestants at the stake. She's stirring up hatred and fighting. My ma and pa are dead because of her."

Thoughts of that terrible night rushed through his mind.

The friendly gathering at the Southwark meeting house. Ma smiling as she read a favorite bible story aloud. Then, the sudden blast of muskets. The soldiers setting the roof alight and the meetinghouse going up in flames. The vicar, frantic to save the screaming people. Pa lifting Ben and pushing him through the high window. Ben trying to climb back in and rescue his parents.

Finally, Queen Mary's soldiers shouting, "Good riddance, stinking Protestants!"

His heart ached.

He still had the burn scars on his hands.

He'd never seen Ma and Pa again.

Later, he learned that angry rebels marched through Southwark, planning to dethrone Bloody Mary and crown Princess Elizabeth queen in her place. But Queen Mary's soldiers opened fire on them, and countless people were killed.

"Queen Mary is a monster," Ben said. "No wonder so many hate her."

"Quiet!" Tim said darkly. "You don't want to end up a prisoner, too. No one ever escapes the Tower of London."

CHAPTER FOUR

A sickle moon rose in the evening sky. After the storm, it felt eerily calm. Ben and Tim reached the coal shed after the day's rounds. Ben was quiet and unsettled.

"I'm starving," Tim said. "We didn't even catch a fish for tea. Or an eel."

"Maybe the baker can spare us a stale loaf."

They ran down the winding, cobbled streets, only to find the bakery closed for the night. Noses pressed to the window, they stared longingly at the round, glistening pies.

"I feel like a steak and kidney pie," Ben said.

"That's odd." Tim grinned. "You don't look like one."

Ben rolled his eyes. "Funny, aren't you? Just look at them all—shepherd's pie, partridge pie, swan pie, apple pie, and steak and kidney pie. Which do you want?"

Tim licked his lips. "If I ever get my teeth into a shepherd's pie, I'll think I've died and gone to heaven."

Slowly, they wandered back to the shed.

Stomach growling, Ben crawled under his blanket in the coal shanty's far corner. He still wore his coarse trousers and woolen coat, but they were damp, and he shivered.

At least he had a dry place to sleep. The coalman also gave Ben and Tim one meal a day as payment for delivering coal. Ben felt lucky to have found work and shelter. Hundreds of orphans lived and starved on London's cold streets. He felt lucky to have Tim. Without his parents, Tim had become his family.

All night, he tossed and turned with thoughts of Ma and Pa, Princess Elizabeth, and Queen Mary.

Dawn came, chilly and overcast. Shivering, Ben and Tim warmed their boots at a small fire. Still half asleep, they wolfed down the bread, pickled oysters, and a small jar of ale the coalman had left for them. At least now Ben's stomach didn't hurt quite so much.

London's many church bells began ringing the hour.

Cling-clang, cling-clang.

The best friends fed Muriel the mule her hay. As Ben shoveled coal into the cart, he hummed a nursery rhyme his ma taught him:

> Oranges and lemons
> Say the bells of St. Clements
> You owe me five farthings
> Say the bells of St. Martins
> When will you pay me?
> Say the bells of Old Bailey
> When I grow rich

Say the bells of Shoreditch
And when will that be?
Say the bells of Stepney
Oh, I do not know
Says the great bell of Bow.
Here comes a candle
To light you to bed
And here comes a chopper
To chop off your head!

Life had been good when Pa and Ma were alive.
They'd lived in a pretty cottage along the River Thames.
Pa caught fish to sell in the market. Ma kept a fire
burning and baked fresh fish or sheep trotters for tea.
How he'd loved those sheep trotters.

"Ready to hitch up the cart?" Tim asked.

"I'll hold Muriel steady."

With Muriel hitched up, they set off. Small children with scabby heads clustered around him in the street, holding out thin arms and begging for food. Ben was still chewing his chunk of dry bread, but he handed it over.

The happy children scampered away.

He and Tim would have to catch a fish if they wanted to eat tonight.

At least he had a job and a home. Delivering coal wasn't bad. Better than working for a chimney sweep as a climbing boy. Imagine squeezing up a narrow, sooty chimney. Working for a gong farm would be even worse; jumping into stinky cesspools filled with poop all day long? By St. George, that would be awful!

Being an orphan was hard. Even orphaned Princess Elizabeth had it bad. And she was an heir to England's throne!

He swung himself up into the cart next to Tim. "How about you deliver St. Paul's Cross their coal today? I can do the Tower rooms."

Tim shot him a wary glance. "Got a plan, have you? Watch out, no messing around with princesses."

Ben rolled his eyes. "Princesses wouldn't mess around with coal boys." He shoved his hair out of his eyes. "How old do you think Princess Elizabeth is?"

"I don't know," Tim said. "Why?"

"Just asking." Ben hunched lower against the cold.

Buildings sagged inward, framing the tunnel-like lane. If they sagged any further, their roofs would touch. Muriel clip-clopped lazily over the cobbled stones.

"Come on, Muriel, old girl, move!" Tim shouted. "Don't wiffle-waffle."

Muriel just snorted.

Ben chuckled. It was impossible to make the grumpy mule move faster.

When they neared London Bridge, a crowd slowed them further. A big gathering at this hour? How strange. Street vendors and beggars were talking in frantic voices.

Tim let out a strangled cry.

"What?" Ben bolted upright. "What's wrong?"

Speechless, Tim just pointed.

And then Ben saw them: the heads, impaled on spikes. He almost threw up.

"Zooks!" he gasped. "What happened?"

"I don't know," Tim said. "It's horrible. Don't look at them."

A newsboy waved a fistful of newspapers. "Read about the Wyatt Rebellion. Sir Thomas Wyatt arrested! Rebels' heads on spikes! Read all about it!"

Ben beckoned the newsboy. "What happened?"

"It's the rebels," the newsboy reported with relish. "Queen Mary ordered them executed." He waved his newsheet at the crowd. "Read about the plot against Queen Mary! Read about the Wyatt Rebellion! Ninety arrested for treason! Princess Elizabeth locked up!"

Ben caught the newsboy's arm. "How many have been executed?"

"About forty, last count. And more to come. The Queen doesn't mess around." He waved the newsheet. "Read all about it!"

"Can I take a quick look?" Ben reached out, suddenly

glad his ma had taught him to read. He had to see if there was news of the Princess.

"No reading without paying."

"Just a quick look," Ben begged.

Reluctantly, the newsboy held out the newsheet, keeping a close grip on the paper.

Ben scanned it as fast as he could, skipping some big words.

"What's it say?" Tim leaned over, struggling to look.

"Sir Thomas Wyatt tried to overthrow Queen Mary and crown Princess Elizabeth queen instead."

"How?"

"Through a marriage plot. If Princess Elizabeth married her second cousin, the Earl of Devon, they'd be crowned king and queen, and Bloody Mary would lose her throne. But the marriage was stopped."

"Zooks! So that's why the Princess has been arrested," Tim said. "Are they going to execute her?"

The newsboy snatched the newsheet away. "No more reading without paying."

"What else did the newsheet say?" Tim asked.

"Princess Elizabeth didn't even know about the marriage plot," Ben said. "She had nothing to do with it! It wasn't her fault. She's innocent."

"Well, of course she says that," Tim scoffed. "She doesn't want her head to get chopped off."

"Queen Mary must really hate her half-sister now," Ben said.

CHAPTER FIVE

LONDON BRIDGE

As they crossed London Bridge and headed for the Tower, Ben tried not to look at the grisly spiked heads. Instead, he scanned the Tower's fifteen-foot thick, high walls and many gatehouses manned by armed guards. No one escaped those men.

The mule-cart clattered over the drawbridge. Below, the moat churned, its water dark brown with poop. Ben held his nose and tried not to inhale.

"I wouldn't want to try and escape by swimming through that."

"Yeah," Tim agreed. "Yuck. Everyone who's lived in the Tower has emptied their chamber pots into that moat. Even old William the Conqueror's poo is drifting around in there."

"Blech!"

"Anyway," Tim said. "Who said anything about escaping? The only way to escape the Tower is the hangman's rope or the executioner's ax. You better not be thinking about helping the Princess."

"I'm not." Ben studied the murder holes over the arches. They were called murder holes because guards could pour boiling oil or molten lead through them onto escaping prisoners—or, in older times, on invaders.

Once inside the walls, he passed the menagerie: the caged lions roared and a wolf howled. Jackdaws and ravens screeched and swooped overhead.

The boys crossed a grassy lawn with buildings on all sides. Troops stood on the green in formation, their pikes, steel caps, and armor glittering in the pale sunlight.

Martial music blared. The Queen's banners blew in the wind. Archers marched atop the walls. The canons, ordinarily unmanned, now buzzed with men at the ready.

"Looks like Queen Mary's frightened," Ben whispered. "She probably thinks the people will rise up and help Princess Elizabeth take the throne. Then they'd throw *her* in the Tower instead. Serve her right."

"I wouldn't want to be royal," Tim whispered. "You'd have to watch your back."

Ben pulled on the reins and said, "Halt, Muriel."

Muriel came to a sudden halt, nearly throwing the boys from the cart.

Ben jumped out and hoisted a coal bucket. "Won't be long."

Tim said, "Come straight back."

Ben walked fast to the White Tower entrance. On the

lawn they called the Tower Green, the wooden scaffold where Queen Anne Boleyn was beheaded still stood in place, waiting for its next victim.

Ben sure hoped the Princess hadn't seen that.

At the door, four barrel-chested Beefeaters blocked his way. The yeoman warders, dressed in high, broad-brimmed hats and crimson cloaks with ruffled collars, looked Ben up and down. There were a lot of new men today, but one face was familiar.

The man smiled a greeting. "Good morning, young Forrester."

Ben smiled back. "Good morning, sir. Any new prisoners needing coal today?"

"Just the same old prisoners in the White Tower, and they're all set." He pointed toward the Bell Tower. "Three new arrivals over there, though. One on the second floor, and two on the third. Follow me."

The Beefeater led Ben to the Bell Tower. On the ground floor, he removed three keys from an iron hoop and handed them to Ben. "My old knees don't want to climb up that steep stairway. Make sure you bring the keys straight back, lad."

Until today, Ben had never thought much about being handed those keys. Now, it was different. One key belonged to the Princess's chamber!

Ben climbed the spiral stairway. The Bell Tower smelled of mold. He blinked to adjust his eyes to the gloom, one hand clutching his heavy bucket, the other on the damp stone wall.

From somewhere, a voice cried out, followed by maniacal laughing; a prisoner gone mad. Ben didn't

know what crime he'd committed, but he was sorry
for him.

On the second-floor landing, he knocked on a thick
oak door. When no one answered, he unlocked the door.
On the chamber's far wall, a barred window let in
gray light. The room was dank with a low ceiling. A thin

mattress lay along one wall. Along another, a writing desk held a quill and ink, and a water jar. Wind whistled through the window.

The place was freezing.

A small figure sat alone, wrapped in a blue cloak with a fur-lined hood. Shoulders hunched, she faced the empty hearth and shivered. From her tangled red curls, Ben knew it was her: Princess Elizabeth.

"Good morning, Your Highness," Ben said. "I've brought coal. You'll be able to warm up."

"I have coal." The Princess didn't look at him. "But I don't know how to get it to burn."

"I'll fix that." Ben hurried forward. While he couldn't help her escape, this was something he *could* do for her.

Ben stacked twigs and set them alight. As the twigs began to crackle, he added a shovel of coal. The fire caught fast.

Instantly, the whole room looked much better.

"Thank you," Princess Elizabeth said, moving so close to the hearth that she was almost sitting in the brightly burning fire.

Ben rubbed his icy hands. "I'll bring more coal tomorrow."

The Princess finally glanced up. "Oh! You're not a guard."

"No, I'm a coal boy."

She stared. "You were at the Traitor's Gate."

"Yes, Your Highness," Ben said, surprised she recognized him. "I'm sorry I couldn't help you. I wish I could."

"I know, I could see that, thank you." Dark shadows under her eyes showed that she hadn't slept. Being a

29

prisoner in the Tower would keep even the strongest person awake. She said, "Please, I'd hate for you to be punished for calling me Your Highness. I'm simply Madame Elizabeth here."

"I'm Ben," he blurted.

"Hello, Ben."

He didn't know what else to say. He cleared his throat awkwardly. "I'll come back tomorrow to help with your fire."

She nodded, and although she smiled, he saw terror in her dark eyes.

Ben felt awful locking the door. He swallowed hard. What a gloomy place. The poor Princess!

It was late afternoon by the time he and Tim, black with coal dust, headed toward home.

They neared a courtyard where a large crowd was cheering at a cockfight. A tall man in a floppy black hat with a yellow feather broke free and dashed toward them.

Ben pulled on the reins. "Whoa, Muriel old girl! Whoa."

The boys held on tight as the mule stopped dead, nearly throwing them clear as usual.

The stranger wore black-velvet pantaloons with fancy slashes that showed off yellow satin underneath. This he'd paired with a velvet doublet and a black cloak.

Ben shot Tim a puzzled glance. Rich men like this never approached the coal cart. Still, this one looked vaguely familiar. Then Ben remembered where he'd seen him: at the watergate yesterday morning when they'd locked up the Princess!

The man pressed a coin into Ben's hand. "M-m-meet me in the alley behind the P-P-Pig and Whistle Tavern," he stuttered, shaking his head twice to the right with an odd nervous twitch.

Ben peeked down at his hand. A shiny coin gleamed. "Yes, sir!"

The man darted away.

Tim looked dubious. "Sounds like trouble."

"I'm going. I want to see what he wants," Ben said.

"Fopdoodles who hand over shiny coins always spell trouble," Tim said.

Ben shrugged. "Can't hurt to see what it's about."

He climbed down and walked cautiously into the dark alley. The rich man stood in the shadows. After looking both ways to make sure no one was watching, he handed Ben a basket. Inside lay two ball-shaped objects wrapped in paper.

"O-oranges," the man said. "A g-g-gift for Princess Elizabeth, coal boy. When you deliver her coal, make sure she gets this. I'll g-g-give you two more coins, same time here tomorrow."

"I can't take messages to the Princess, sir," Ben said. "The warders would never allow it."

"No m-m-messages." The man twitched his head twice, unwrapped an orange, and showed Ben the blank paper. "Just oranges, so she won't get ill. P-p-prisoners can receive food. Surely you don't b-b-begrudge doing that?"

"Of course not, sir. I'll bring her the oranges first thing."

The oranges seemed innocent enough. Still, he had a

bad feeling about this. Something told him he was being tricked.

"What's your name?" Ben asked the strange man.

He didn't answer. Instead, he darted away into the shadows and was gone.

CHAPTER SIX

LONDON
THE NEXT DAY

T he following day, Ben and Tim crossed Tower Bridge once again. This time, the suspicious basket of oranges lay at Ben's feet. He couldn't look at the heads on spikes; now, they terrified him.

What was he getting himself into?

Was the stuttering man one of Sir Thomas Wyatt's rebels? If so, he might be trying to help the Princess escape. Ben would be happy about that. But as the heads on spikes stared down, nervous sweat trickled down his sides.

If he were caught for treason, Bloody Mary would have his head chopped off.

Ben picked up the oranges, remembering how his father had used his last breath to push him out of that window. His father had given his life to save Ben—and now he was afraid of delivering some fruit?

Princess Elizabeth was the only person capable of stopping Bloody Mary from terrorizing England. He raised his chin and dug up his courage.

At the Bell Tower entrance, the Beefeater examined the basket's contents while Ben's knees shook.

"Go on," the man said, handing him the keys.

Ben sagged with relief.

Inside, the Princess sat hunched by the empty grate. She glanced up as he entered.

"Ben," she said.

"Madame Elizabeth, I have a gift for you." Ben held out the basket. "Oranges, Your Highness, from a nobleman."

"Please, keep them. I have no appetite."

Ben whispered, "You might want to take a closer look, My Lady."

Her eyes widened.

Nervous, Ben glanced over his shoulder, knowing he could end up dead. "I think the nobleman sent you a message."

Princess Elizabeth whispered, "A message?"

"Yes."

"From who?"

"I don't know. A nobleman with a stutter."

She took the oranges and unfurled the wrapping. "There's no message here."

"I think I know why. Let me try something." Ben piled coal into the fireplace. When it was burning brightly, he said, "Watch for the guard. And hand me the paper."

She did.

He held the wrapping paper to the heat.

"What are you doing?" she asked, curious.

"The paper looks empty, but there might be more than meets the eye. My ma taught me a game using invisible ink. You write the words in orange juice, and it's invisible." He waved the paper. "Until you heat it up. Then, the letters appear."

"How wonderful," the Princess said, leaning close.

Together, they stared at the paper.

Nothing.

"There's no message," the Princess said, her eyes clouded with defeat.

Determined, Ben held the paper near the flames until his fingers were scorching hot.

Suddenly, like magic, words appeared. By St. George! It was just as he'd suspected!

"It worked!" he hissed. "Look, instructions for an escape plan!"

Princess Elizabeth grabbed the message. Her eyes shone with excitement. "Please, God, let this be true."

Ben said, "I hope that man was trustworthy."

Princess Elizabeth gave an excited laugh. "He is. You said he had a stutter? That could only be Sir Edward Courtenay, the Earl of Devon."

The Earl of Devon? The man from the marriage plot?

She said, "He is very kind, even if he is a little odd. He got that way because he spent fifteen years in the Tower. His father was executed for treason against my father, King Henry. Poor Edward was only twelve when he and his mother were imprisoned. He's my second cousin. He's very close in line to the throne."

Ben felt a sliver of unease. It sounded unsafe to be close in line to the throne. It sounded deadly. And why was the Earl of Devon still free? Why hadn't Mary locked him up, too?

Princess Elizabeth whispered, "It was dangerous to bring me this message. Why did you do it?"

"Because I want to help you, Your Highness." Ben looked at the floor. "My ma and pa said you are England's true queen."

"I am but a prisoner now."

The guard's heavy footsteps sounded outside the door.

"Hurry," she said, "You must go before they suspect you of helping me."

She was right. He shouldn't be in here talking to the Princess like this! He picked up his coal bucket and hurried for the door. As he locked her inside, he said, "I will pray for you, Your Highness."

"Thank you, Ben."

He bowed. "God be with you." Then he turned the key in the lock and went about his rounds.

He'd done his duty. Now he could breathe easier. The Earl of Devon would help his cousin escape, they could be married and claim the throne, and Ben had done the right thing. Even if it was hard to imagine those two getting married!

As Muriel clattered over the drawbridge, Ben could still see the writing in his mind.

The plan was simple:

Two of Princess Elizabeth's ladies-in-waiting and a maid would visit her. The Princess and the maid would exchange clothes. Then, dressed as the maid, she and the ladies would leave the Tower. Her supporters would be waiting in a carriage outside the Sally Port drawbridge. They'd head to the harbor and sail to France.

It was a brave plan, especially for the maid who got left behind.

But so many were willing to risk their lives to fight for Elizabeth and rid England of Bloody Queen Mary. And when Elizabeth was Queen, she'd free the maid.

What terrible times they were living in.

That evening, he went to meet the Earl again. Tense, he waited in the alley behind the Pig and Whistle. Someone grabbed him and yanked him into the shadows. He shouted, but a hand closed over his mouth.

"Quiet boy, do you want us to get caught?" It was the Earl. "Did you d-d-deliver the oranges?"

Ben nodded. "Aye."

The Earl slipped two coins into his hand.

Clutching the shiny coins, Ben went to join Tim. "I'm glad that's done."

"Did that twitching nobleman pay you?"

"Yes, we'll eat well tonight. He was crafty. When he sent the oranges, he was sending an invisible message in orange juice. Have you ever seen invisible writing?"

Wide-eyed, Tim shook his head.

Ben told him about writing in orange juice and how heat made the writing appear.

"Like a magic trick!" Tim said.

"Exactly." Ben's stomach growled. With three shiny coins, he felt positively wealthy. They ran for the pie shop. Ben bought himself a steak and kidney pie and a shepherd's pie. Tim did the same.

Ben took a huge bite, swallowed, and smacked his lips. "That's good!"

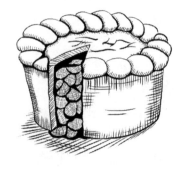

Gravy running down his chin, Tim agreed. "I'll bet they eat Shepherd's pie in heaven. I knew it would be delicious, and I was right. So, tell me again about that magic writing. The heat really made the message appear? I've never heard of that."

"The Princess didn't know about it either." Ben was starting to feel good. He'd helped the Princess and earned some money. He counted the remaining change coins in his hand.

"Where'd you get those?" The voice was harsh.

Ben glanced up into a stern-looking copper's red face.

"I—I worked for it."

Tim poked his back, hard.

Nervous, Ben dropped a coin.

As it rolled across the cobbles, a ferret-faced man darted out of a doorway, snatched it up, and ran.

"Hoy!" The copper ran after him.

Holding tight to their pies, Ben and Tim ran too—in the opposite direction. Back in the coal shed, they ate slowly, enjoying every juicy morsel.

"What did the invisible message say?" Tim asked. "What did the twitching man write?"

Ben shook his head, "Better not to talk about it."

He thought of the escape plan and prayed nothing went wrong.

CHAPTER SEVEN

LONDON
THE NEXT MORNING

Ben loaded up the coal cart the following morning, wondering if the escape plan was underway.

Maybe it was done, and Princess Elizabeth was gone.

If so, the place would be in an uproar. Ben would have to hide his grin and pretend he knew nothing.

Yet strangely, after clip-clopping through the Tower's thick walls, they found everything calm and quiet. She must have gotten clean away, and the guards still thought the disguised maid was the Princess!

Ben approached the Bell Tower.

A guard stood with his muscular arms folded across his chest. "Good day, young Forrester. Brought the coal early, did you?"

Ben gulped, tried to smile. "Yes!"

"Madame Elizabeth seems a bit down this morning.

She hasn't gotten out of bed. Maybe a warm fire in the grate will help."

"Yes, I'm sure it will."

So, the maid was hiding under the blankets. Good plan.

"Don't dally." The guard handed him the hoop of keys.

In the spiral stairway, the only light came from arrow slits in the thick walls. He reached the second floor and peered through the barred window.

A young woman knelt by a chair, her face in her hands as though praying. Ben thought he heard a strangled sob. Feeling embarrassed, he knocked on the door before putting the key in the lock.

"I'm just here with the coal," he said and went inside.

The girl sat up quickly, scrubbing her red eyes and nose. "Oh! Ben. Hello."

"Madame Elizabeth, it's you!" he cried.

"Yes."

"What about the Earl's plan? It didn't work?"

"Unfortunately, my sister the Queen sent orders to stop me from having any visitors."

Startled, Ben said, "Do you think she suspected you?"

"Maybe," the Princess said, "I don't know how, but maybe someone told her. My ladies were turned away."

A breeze whistled through the barred window. Elizabeth's face was pale and splotchy beneath her tangled red curls. No one had ever looked so alone. Not the beggars in the street—not even the alley cats, for at least they were free.

"Who would have told her?" Ben eventually said, kneeling to make the fire.

"I don't know. But it gets worse." She came to stand by him, and her mouth trembled. "This morning, my cousin, Lady Jane Gray, was beheaded. *Beheaded!* For treason. She was only sixteen! Her husband, too. Both of them had their heads chopped off right outside, on the Tower Green. Just like my poor mother." She pressed her shaking fingers to her lips, swallowed hard. "How could Mary do this? Jane was her cousin."

Horrified, Ben said, "Kill her own family?"

"I fear I'm next. All Mary thinks of is her throne. She doesn't care who she kills, as long as she can keep her crown on her head. She terrorizes the good people of England, and she hates that I'm her sister—to her, I'm

42

not a relative, I'm a nuisance. And she can't wait to send me to the chopping block."

Ben didn't know what to say.

Her eyes had grown damp. She went to the writing table and sank onto the chair. "She's murdering my friends. Sir Thomas Wyatt is in the torture chamber as we speak. And there's nothing I can do to help him!" Picking up the inkpot, she flung it at the wall. A tear spilled down her cheek, and she scrubbed it away.

"What do the torturers want him to say?" Ben asked.

She sank down. "That I tried to marry my cousin in the Wyatt Rebellion and steal her throne. But I didn't! I only heard of the plot when they arrested me. My sister longs to call me a traitor so she can execute me. And I feel sick, thinking of my friend being tortured."

Ben felt desperate and angry. This was so wrong!

She licked her chapped lips. "I don't have long on this earth. They're taking me to Westminster to be tried for treason." Her face had gone waxen with fear. "It's likely I'll be convicted and executed within days."

Ben's heart missed a beat.

The next time he delivered coal, the Princess—this girl who had become a friend—could have her head on a spike on London Bridge. Rotting in the sunshine. He couldn't bear it.

"I'll help you escape," he blurted.

His words clearly startled them both.

After a shocked moment of silence, the Princess said, "That's kind, but there's nothing you can do." She wrinkled her brow. "Is there?"

"Same plan," Ben said, thinking fast. "We'll exchange

clothes. We're almost the same height, and we're both skinny. You can hide your red curls under my cap. We'll smudge your face and hands with chimney soot. Then, you just have to walk out with my coal bucket."

Her eyes went round with hope. "But—"

Ben went on. "Below, you'll see a coal cart waiting. Climb into it. My friend Tim is down there, waiting. He'll be shocked and scared when he sees you, but he won't betray you. Tell him where your cousin, the Earl of Devon, lives, and he'll take you there."

"But what about you?" the Princess said.

"Don't worry about me. I know my way around." Ben raised the keys. "And I can open doors." He tried not to think of the many ways the plan could go wrong.

"If you're caught, they'll execute you," the Princess said. "I can't let you do it."

"They won't catch me. Now hurry before a guard opens the door."

He turned away and pulled off his coat. Behind him, he could hear the rustle of the Princess undressing. Trying not to look, he reached back with his clothes. In exchange, he got an armful of lace-trimmed dress and flounced petticoat.

He stared at the dress and realized the first fault in his plan. How could he escape in this?

"Do you have a plain sort of gown?" he said. "And a big cloak with a hood?"

"One moment." He heard her footsteps, what sounded like a chest opening, and then some rustling. She handed him a gray gown with puffed sleeves and a navy cloak with a fur-lined hood.

Ben pulled on the dress, sniffing the faint perfume. He'd never smelled like roses before. Too bad he hadn't washed his *own* clothes in days. No way they'd smell like roses.

"You may turn around," the Princess said.

There she stood in his coal-stained coat, woolen trousers, and cap. She looked like a thin, pale boy who worked for the chimney sweeps.

"Whoa!" he said. "You could fool me."

She cocked her head. "But you don't quite look like a girl. Pull your hood up."

He did and said, "You still need one finishing touch." Quickly, he smeared soot over her cheeks, down her nose, and over the curls jutting from his cap.

"Better?" she asked.

"Yes. Keep your head down." He pulled the brown cap lower on her forehead so that it shaded her face. "Don't look at anyone. Walk downstairs and straight out the entrance. If a warder speaks to you, pretend you don't hear. I'll give you ten minutes, and then I'll get out. A crowd often visits the animal menagerie at this hour. I'll hide and leave with them."

She nodded.

This was really going to work!

Face tense, the Princess took the coal bucket. "You're very brave to help me. Thank you. I'll never forget this, Ben."

Ben gave a sheepish nod. He felt like a nincompoop dressed in a long dark-gray dress with puffed sleeves and a cloak. If Tim saw him now, he'd die of laughter.

"What's your last name, Ben?" she asked.

"Forrester, My Lady. And don't forget, my friend's name is Tim. Tell him to take you over the Sally Port drawbridge. It's the best way, as it bypasses the guards at the main gate."

She nodded, her eyes bright. "May God bless you, Ben Forrester. May he bless us both." She undid the clasp of her pearl necklace and pressed it into his hand. "Take this. It's for you."

"Thank you, Your Highness," Ben whispered.

As she left, he prayed she wouldn't run into a warder in the stairwell. If a guard spoke to her, it would be over.

Listening to her fading footsteps, he whispered, "Go with God."

When the tower fell silent, his heart began to hammer in earnest. He was alone in a dress, and he'd helped the Princess escape. He forced himself to stay in place and count the minutes she'd need. Still, every fiber of his body urged him to make a break for it, to run as if the hounds of hell were at his heels.

Two minutes passed, enough for her to get down the stairs.

Another two minutes—she'd be walking past the guards.

Another minute—she'd be finding Tim and climbing into the cart.

Five minutes now—Tim would be driving the cart across the drawbridge.

But what if good old Muriel had stopped to munch grass? What if she'd refused to budge until she'd finished?

Cold sweat poured down his sides. He needed to get out before a warder came.

He started at a sudden sound. Someone was outside the door.

Racing across the room, Ben dove into the bed and hauled the blanket over his body.

His heart thumped like a drum. He wanted to charge the stairs, or puke, or both.

This was bad.

Very bad.

CHAPTER EIGHT

THE TOWER OF LONDON
M0MENTS LATER

T he heavy oak door creaked open.

Ben lay like a cornered mouse. He prayed the guard would think he was the Princess, fast asleep.

Heavy footsteps thumped across the stone floor.

Ben's heart pounded in his ears.

"Madame Elizabeth," a deep voice said. "I have your midday meal here."

Fists clenched, Ben pressed his face into the mattress.

The footsteps drew closer. A hand yanked back Ben's hood, and a surprised shout rang out.

"Who are you? What are you doing in Madame Elizabeth's bed?"

"I—I—"

"Where's Madame Elizabeth?" The guard scanned the room, his eyes frantic.

Ben tried for an I-don't-know-what-you're-talking-about expression.

The burly guard hauled Ben out from under the blanket and shook Ben so hard that his teeth rattled. "Answer me! Where's the Princess?"

"I don't know!"

Face purple, the guard shoved Ben back onto the mattress, and raced out of the room.

"Warder! Warder!" the guard shouted. "Raise the drawbridges! Alert the guards! Madame Elizabeth has escaped!"

Tower bells began to peal, clanging the alarm.

Footsteps thundered as warders and sentries swarmed up and down the stairwells, searching for the Princess.

Ben cowered when his door flew open again, and three Beefeaters stormed into the room.

"Where is Madame Elizabeth?" a hawk-faced Beefeater said.

"I don't know, sir," Ben stammered.

"What were you doing in her bed?"

Ben's mind scrambled for some possible explanation. "The cell was empty when I entered. I was bringing coal, sir. I felt a bit queasy, and I lay down. I must have fainted."

Not bad for a last-minute excuse!

But the Beefeater was unimpressed. He stuck his big, red nose right up to Ben's. "Why are you wearing Madame Elizabeth's clothing?"

Ben looked down at the dark-gray dress. Zooks! How could he ever explain this? Maybe he should pretend he'd lost his mind. Maybe he had. What could he say? He'd helped a prisoner escape. Not just any prisoner. A princess. The half-sister and rival to the Bloody Queen.

Sick with fear, he clutched his head. "I'm confused! I don't know."

The hawk-faced Beefeater glowered at him. "Confused, hey? Methinks someone paid you to help the prisoner escape. You'd better confess, or it will go worse for you. Who paid you? What do you know of Sir Thomas Wyatt's Rebellion against the Queen?"

Ben's throat went dry with fear. "No one paid me."

"Are you working for Wyatt?"

"I'm just a coal boy, sir."

"Sir Thomas Wyatt is in the Tower. He'll be tortured until he reveals the names of every traitor," the hawk-faced Beefeater growled.

"He won't reveal my name. I don't know him!" At least that was true.

"Confess, boy, or I'll stretch you on the rack until you do. Who are you working for?"

The rack? Frozen with terror, Ben's brain went numb. "No one, sir."

"What is your name? Who are your parents?"

"My name is Ben Forrester."

"I asked who your parents are."

"I'm an orphan, sir."

"You better tell the truth fast, Ben Forrester. Or the Constable of the Tower will help you remember who paid you."

The Beefeaters stormed out.

Still reeling, Ben staggered to the small window. Below, guards swarmed the grounds. Had Princess Elizabeth found Tim and escaped? Or was Tim now a prisoner, too? What if he'd endangered his best friend?

Clinging to the bars, he tried to come up with a plan.

They were going to torture him.

What if he babbled about delivering the oranges with the invisible message?

He had to escape.

He still had the keys, which he'd shoved under the mattress earlier. But if he tried the halls, he'd get nowhere in this dress now. Could he loosen the window bars and scale down to the fortress wall-top? He peered out. He'd need a rope; he'd never survive the jump. And if he did, he'd still have to cross the stinky moat.

He'd heard that a prisoner once tried to escape by rope. The Welsh prince lowered himself from the roof, but the rope broke, and he plunged to his death.

Still, it was a smart idea—if he'd had stronger equipment.

A desperate idea came to him. Maybe Tim could deliver him a rope inside a bucket of coal? Could he ask that of his friend?

No, the rope he'd need would never fit inside a bucket.

But what if . . . Yes—that could work!

The oranges, paper, and quill still lay on the writing desk. Could he send Tim a secret message? But who would deliver it? And would Tim remember about the invisible ink?

Even if Tim got the message, he couldn't read.

Well, Ben would write the message in pictures.

He bit into an orange, squeezed out some juice, and dipped the quill. Quickly, he started to sketch.

First, he drew Tim, a stick figure with bowlegs, placing not a rope but a fishing line in a coal bucket. Second, he drew Tim handing the coal bucket to a stick man in a warder's hat. Ben drew a third and fourth sketch to complete his complete escape plan. It would be difficult and risky, but it was the best he could think up.

If only he could give Tim a definite day and time!

Instead, he drew the moon in the sky, with two sun rays peeking out over the horizon. He hoped Tim would guess the escape would take place in the darkness before dawn.

Ben wrapped the finished sketch around an orange. Hopefully, Tim would remember their talk about invisible messages.

Mustering his courage, he knocked on the oak door.

A guard unlocked it and peered in. Ben's heart leaped. He was the friendly man with big, brown eyes. They'd chatted just yesterday.

The guard's eyes crinkled. "Right funny you look, lad. Why are you wearing a dress?"

"It's difficult to explain," Ben said, his face hot. He cleared his throat. "Sir, I want to send an orange to my friend Tim. You know him, sir, he delivers coal to the Tower. Could you please give him this orange from me?" His voice was coming out all squeaky.

The man shook his head. "Sorry, lad. I haven't been told what's going on here, but I can't take messages."

"It's not a message, sir," Ben said. Desperate, he tried to look innocent and sincere. "Tim and I are like brothers. He is an orphan like me. He's probably waiting for me in the coal cart, and he'll be wondering what's happened. If you tell him the orange is from me, he'll know I am alright. You needn't give him any messages, sir." He unwrapped the paper to show that it was blank. Then he handed over the second orange. "And here is an orange for you, sir. Very tasty, they are."

The guard looked hesitant. "Where did these come from?"

"A . . . a customer gave them to me this morning, sir. On my rounds," Ben lied.

"They're expensive. You'd best keep them for yourself."

"Oranges make me turn out in an itchy rash, sir. I meant to give them to the Princess. Take them. Please?"

Oranges were a rare, luxury fruit, and they cost a lot. The guard stretched out his hand. "If I see Tim, I'll give him his orange. I'll take the other one for my ma. And I'll ask her to say a prayer for you, lad. You'll need as many prayers as you can get."

"Thank you, sir."

"I don't know what you thought you were doing. Perhaps you fancied that pretty Princess. You're in a terrible mess." He shook his head. "I feel sorry for you, lad."

"I'm grateful, sir." Ben felt a wave of relief. This guard was kind and might help him. "Did the Princess escape, then?"

The guard lowered his voice. "No. They found her hiding in the stairwell. The Constable of the Tower is questioning her now."

Ben's heart sank.

It had all been for nothing.

"Thank you for telling me," Ben said.

The guard nodded and left, locking the door.

Alone and ice cold with fear, he went to the window. A raven, its black wings gleaming, swooped across the sky.

How Ben longed to be free.

CHAPTER NINE

Later that afternoon, the friendly guard returned with a bucket of coal.

Eagerly, Ben took it. "Did my friend, Tim, get the orange?"

"The freckle-faced lad. Yes. He was waiting for you at the Bell Tower entrance. I told him you were in trouble and gave him the orange. Poor lad looked worried sick. He left and came back with this bucket of coal for you. He thought you'd be cold; seems a storm is expected tonight."

Ben almost whooped in relief.

So, the plan was in motion—if Tim had remembered the invisible writing trick.

"Thank you, sir," he said. "Did your ma enjoy her orange?"

The guard grinned. "Yes, I went to my ma's for tea. She said it was the best thing she'd ever tasted. I also grabbed you some of my clothes. Thought you may wish to change out of those petticoats." He handed Ben a worn woolen shirt, a tunic, and trousers.

"Thank you so much, sir," Ben said, grateful he had found at least one kind guard.

When the warder left, Ben set to work, praying Tim had figured out the note. He shoveled coal into the grate, not stopping until the bucket was empty.

Yes! At the bottom lay a fishing line. By St. George, Tim understood. Plus, Ben had proper men's clothing. The plan could work!

But he wasn't out of the woods yet.

Somehow, he had to get to the Tower roof. Once up there, he'd wait for Tim to appear on the moat's far side. Then he'd attach a stone to the fishing line and throw it to Tim. Once Tim caught it, Tim would attach a thick rope to the fishing line, and Ben would haul it up. At that point, Ben would slide down the rope to Tim's side, and they'd run like the blazes.

He buzzed with excitement. He'd be out of this place so fast they wouldn't know what hit them. Take that, mean old hawk-nose Beefeater!

He pulled off Princess Elizabeth's dress, changed into trousers, and wound the fishing line round and round his waist. Then he pulled the shirt over it. Thank goodness for that kind guard. He'd have a hard time sliding to safety in lace petticoats!

Once dressed, Ben fetched the pearl necklace from the table. He wished he could give it to Ma—her eyes would have gone round as saucers. How he longed to talk to her. Maybe he'd made a mistake trying to help the Princess. Maybe he'd made everything worse. What would Ma and Pa have done? He heard his ma's voice in his head and knew the answer right away. They would have tried to help her, too.

He was about to shove the necklace into his pocket when the door swung open. The hawk-nose Beefeater glared, and the look on his face was terrifying. What was this about?

Ben shrank away, his fear rising.

"Hands behind your back," the hawk-nose Beefeater said and tied Ben's wrists.

Ben felt sick. What about the plan?

The Beefeater hauled him down the spiral staircase, accompanied by more guards. Lighted torches flickered against the walls. They led him down an unfamiliar maze of endless dark corridors.

Finally, they emerged onto a section of the Tower grounds Ben recognized. He stumbled, his knees weak with fear.

Wakefield Tower, ancient and dark, loomed ahead.

Wakefield Tower, where the torture chamber lay.

He took a deep, shuddering breath.

Inside, the Constable of the Tower, an imposing figure in a tall, black hat and thick black cloak with a white ruff, stood behind a desk. He didn't look up as Ben was dragged in. Instead, he studied the paper in front of him.

"You are Ben Forrester, employed to deliver the Tower's coal?"

"Yes, sir," Ben stammered.

The Constable dipped his quill pen in ink and made a note. "You were seen talking to the Earl of Devon outside the Pig and Whistle Tavern."

Ben stared in shock. He'd been seen? By who?

"What did the Earl ask you to do?" the Constable demanded.

"N-nothing," Ben stuttered.

"Answer the question or face torture."

"The Earl just wanted to know the way to the next tavern," Ben lied.

"Indeed?" The Constable of the Tower looked up. His

eyes were cold as ice. "The Earl handed you a basket of oranges. Why?"

"He asked if I would like them."

"Maybe you'd like to hang from a hook for a while, Ben Forrester, until you decide to tell the truth."

Ben's heart missed a beat.

"The Earl of Devon has been arrested," the Constable said. "He is here in the Tower. We will find out why you were working for him. If you keep lying to us, things will go badly for you. But if you confess now, I will be lenient."

Ben didn't believe that for a minute. His mouth was dry as cotton. "I didn't know he was the Earl of Devon." At least that bit was true.

"What do you know of Sir Thomas Wyatt?" the Constable demanded.

"N-nothing," Ben stammered. "Only what I heard from the newsboy."

The warder tightened the ropes around Ben's wrists until they bit into his skin. Ben's arms were being twisted so hard he gasped.

"What did the Earl of Devon ask you to do?" the Constable demanded.

"Nothing."

"Did Madame Elizabeth talk to you about the Wyatt Rebellion?"

"No."

"Did Madame Elizabeth ask you to help her escape?"

"No."

"What did Princess Elizabeth know of the Wyatt Rebellion?" The Constable's angry voice suggested that he desperately wanted Ben to say the Princess was guilty—a rebel—plotting to destroy the Queen.

"I don't know. I told you, I don't know! I'm just a coal boy." Ben's mouth twisted as he tried not to cry. Somehow, he forced the trembling inside to harden into a dead calm.

"The boy's lying," snarled the hawk-nosed Beefeater. "We found him wearing her dress." The man shoved Ben hard, sending him crashing to the ground.

Wrists bound and unable to catch himself, Ben's jaw hit the floor with an awful crack. Blood filled his mouth as he bit his tongue, and shocks of pain jolted through him.

"Answer, or we'll stretch you on the rack, Forrester," the Beefeater roared. "You'll be twice as tall when we're done with you."

"I don't know anything," Ben muttered, on the verge of passing out.

"A little time in solitary should soften him up," the Constable of the Tower said.

The Beefeater laughed. "Aye, that it will."

"Bring him back in the morning. We'll get the truth out of him."

Two warders yanked Ben up and hauled him down steep, winding stairs. The deeper the stairs went, the more he began to fear. It felt

like they were descending into hell.

If he didn't escape now, he never would.

Ben abruptly stopped walking and sank to his haunches. The startled guards smashed into one another. Using their momentary confusion to break free, he sprinted down the steps.

But he didn't get far. One guard still held his wrists by a rope. The man gave a vicious yank. Ben toppled sideways in the narrow stairwell.

Head over heels he fell, the stone steps hard under his bones.

Wham. His left knee thwacked down.

Whump. His right shoulder hit hard.

Crack. His forehead smacked a sharp edge.

The world went black.

CHAPTER TEN

THE TOWER OF LONDON
THE DUNGEON AMONG THE RATS

Ben opened his eyes.

All he could see was black. Pitch-black.

Where was he?

A dungeon?

His head, knees, wrists, and jaw throbbed. Groaning, he struggled to his feet. His skull smashed into the ceiling. With a shout, he lost his balance, but something had hold of his ankle. As he fell, a metallic rattle jangled near his foot.

Zooks! What now?

Ben reached for his leg. They'd chained him to the floor! Frantic, he tried to pull loose.

Ouch.

Metal sliced into his skin, and warm blood oozed. He touched it and raised his fingers to his eyes.

It was terrifyingly dark. Too dark to see.

The walls and ceiling closed in on him. With an awful feeling of claustrophobia, he ran his hands over the earthen walls, trying to find something that might help him break the chain. The furthest corner of the dungeon reeked. Urine and poop. So that's where the toilet was. Great!

How long had he been down here?

He sat and tried to think until the silence grew deafening. Where were the guards? Had they left him to die alone?

He longed to hear a voice.

"Is anyone here?" he called.

Silence.

He shuddered. He was freezing cold and starving. Hunger twisted his stomach. He couldn't remember the last time he'd eaten. Or even had a sip of water. His teeth chattered.

Think, he told himself. *Don't give way to panic. Don't give up. Never ever give up. Think.*

To his astonishment, an odd trickling sound began along the left wall. It sounded like . . . water? Yes, like dripping water. Confused, Ben moved toward it. Soft wetness splashed underfoot. The floor was growing muddy, and soon his boots were soaked. The water was rising.

Ben knew the dungeon flanked the River Thames. Sometimes, at high tide, the riverbank overflowed and flooded the Tower.

As the water rose, an awful thought struck. He could drown.

"Help!" Ben shouted. "Help!"

No answer.

Rustling movements sounded in the far corner. His ears pricked.

"Who's there?"

More rustling.

Ben clenched his fists, ready to defend himself. "Tell me who you are!"

Tiny teeth bit his ankle.

"Hey!" he shouted, kicking out.

Scurrying, chittering echoes filled the dungeon. Tiny *click-click-clicks*, like claws scratching across stone. Another sharp bite.

Rats—they were rats. In horror, he knew this awful place.

Once, during his delivery round, Ben heard the Tower Guards joking about this place: The Dungeon Among the Rats. The dark chamber where rats swam in on the tides and attacked the prisoners.

It was rat-time, and Ben was trapped.

Muscles tense, he squinted into the dark depths. Hungry rats ate human flesh. In the poor street where he lived, women dared not leave their babies alone. Rats sensed the helpless. And here he was chained up, with a bleeding ankle.

He pictured the rats squeaking, "Ooh, a person. All chained up and can't get away. Bleeding, too! Let's have a nice little rat-feast."

A rat dashed up his ankle, sharp little claws scratching his skin.

Ben kicked left and right with his free leg. He stomped, trying to scare the nasty creatures away.

Scrambling little feet announced more rats were coming. A lot more, by the sound of it. Scampering across the floor with gnawing teeth and beady red eyes.

Ben pressed his back to the damp wall and kept stamping.

After what seemed forever, the water receded, taking the rats with it.

Ben heard footsteps. The door opened, and an unfamiliar warder appeared, his face ghoul-like in the glow of a lamp. He set down a jar of water and tossed Ben a hunk of bread.

Tears of relief welled in Ben's eyes. He was so thankful to see a human.

"Sir, how long will I be here?" he stammered.

The lamp swayed. Long shadows leaped across the stone walls. The warder shrugged. "Couldn't say. I 'spose until they want you for questioning."

"Sir, I'm so cold," Ben said. "The floor is wet. And there are rats. Could I please have a pallet to lie on so I can get away from them?"

"A pallet, hey?"

Ben's teeth clacked with cold. "Please? And a blanket?"

"What about a soft pillow and a big jar of ale?" the warder said.

Ben looked at him in surprise. "Yes! Thank you, sir."

The warder snorted with laughter. "I'll be sure and send the Queen your demands."

Ben winced at the sound of the lock.

Pins and needles shot up his chained leg. Chills rolled down his back, and his body felt cold and numb. Total hopelessness smothered him. What could he do? Was perishing the only way to escape the Tower?

And then, like a flash, a desperate plan came to him.

He forced himself to eat the moldy bread and gulped mouthfuls of foul-tasting water. When he'd emptied the empty jug, strength and hope began to flow through him. Despite his bruises, his limbs were sturdy from hauling coal. He could do this. He had to.

He just had to wait for the right moment.

As the hours passed, he lost sense of time. Day and night seemed the same.

Finally, he heard the warder's footsteps.

This was his only chance. His heart boomed. He breathed slowly, trying to calm down. Silently, he lay belly down on the wet floor and sprawled out his arms and legs like a dead man. Head turned to one side, mouth open, he rolled his eyes back.

The warder raised his lamp.

"Hey! You alright?"

Ben stared blank-eyed at the far wall.

The warder nudged him with one booted foot.

Ben forced himself to stay limp and show no reaction. He barely breathed. His eyes threatened to water. He needed to blink. He couldn't hold it much longer.

The warder muttered and nudged him a little harder. Setting his lantern down, the man crouched over Ben, leaning in close. His breath smelled of fish.

This was it. Now!

With all his strength, Ben reared up and head-butted the man. With a crack, his forehead smashed into the warder's nose.

The warder crumpled to the floor, unconscious.

It worked. Yes! It really worked.

Breathing hard, Ben fumbled for the warder's hoop of keys. It took three tries to unlock his leg chain. Once free, he fastened it around the guard's ankle.

That should buy him some time.

Then, he staggered out of the dungeon into the maze of murky corridors.

CHAPTER ELEVEN

Ben turned left and raced past a series of dungeons, all empty. He had to get to the Tower ramparts and signal Tim. But he had no idea which way to go.

The passage ended at a spiral stairway. Up was where he wanted to go, so he took it. At the top, he reached an heavy door. Hands shaking, he tried every key on the bunch. None worked.

Jaw steeled with determination, he sped back the way he'd come.

This time, he took the right fork. Although he was lost, he felt wildly triumphant. He'd tricked the guard and had gotten free. He just had to stay free long enough to find a way out.

Buzzing with tension, Ben hurtled along, ears pricked

and eyes alert. He arrived at a fancy metal gate. Again, he tried the keys. His swollen fingers were clumsy and felt like sausages.

Yes! The third key fit.

Cautiously, he tiptoed inside and found a chamber filled with stone coffins, blank-eyed cherubs, and angels with broken wings. A crypt! Spooky.

Ben hurried through and reached a broad flight of stairs on the far side. At the top, an iron door once again blocked his way. He tried key after key. He'd almost given up when one worked. Hurrah!

Ben peered around the doorframe.

No one about.

What he saw were hundreds of swords, lances, cross-bows, arrows, and even cannons. He was in the Tower Armory, the place for storing weapons! They filled the room from floor to ceiling, all for the taking. Imagine firing his way out with a cannon. But even if he could load one and light it, the walls were four-feet-thick. He'd probably blow himself up.

He ran a finger down a dagger's sharp edge. Thinking he could wave it in defense, he slipped the leather sheath into his boot.

According to the light blazing through the narrow, arched windows, it was still afternoon. He went to one and peered outside: sentries paced Tower Green showing no signs of alarm. No scurrying around searching for an escaped prisoner called Ben Forrester. They hadn't found the guard in the dungeon—yet.

Unfortunately, darkness wouldn't be here for hours. He'd have to hide in here and wait.

As Ben rubbed his swollen hands, he wandered deeper into the Armory. It was gloomier back there and filled with statues.

Wide-eyed, he studied the life-sized figures of England's kings. Zooks, they looked ominous!

Two monarchs from long ago were mounted on armor-clad, wooden horses. With their helmets and long lances, the kings looked lifelike and ready to attack.

King Henry VIII's armor was impossible to miss. It was huge. Ben had once seen the frightening monarch from a distance—he'd looked like a boiled ham with a big red face. The massive suit of armor was almost as wide as it was high. He sniggered at the size of the codpiece. He wished he could show it to Tim. Good old King Henry wanted to impress everyone, but how did he ride a horse wearing a codpiece like that?

The statues were unnerving. Too real.

Ben returned to a bench in the windowed area and basked in the sunbeams.

With an awful jolt, he wondered if he still had his fishing line. He yanked up his shirt and breathed a sigh of relief. There it was, still tied around him like a belt.

But would his plan work? Would Tim understand his message? He wasn't much of an artist. At least Tim had understood enough to send the fishing line in the bucket. Would he get the rest?

Tim was also in danger. If Tim were caught, he'd be in huge trouble. What an awful burden to place on his friend. Especially after Tim had warned him not to try anything.

Exhausted by guilt and fear, he huddled up on the stone bench and fell asleep. He woke to the loud clanging of the Tower curfew bell. A bugle sounded. The Tower gates were closing for the night. Deliverymen, workers, and visitors would leave. The great oak doors would be shut and locked. Drawbridges would be raised. Only guards and prisoners would be locked inside.

He'd wait a little longer and then get to the roof.

Shadows moved on the Armories' walls. Talk about

spooky. He'd heard ghost stories about this room: An invisible demon once jumped from the ceiling and tried to suffocate a warder. Another ghost attempted to strangle a guard. A Beefeater even confirmed the presence of red marks on the man's throat!

The warders were a tough bunch; many were ex-soldiers. If they said ghosts haunted this place, it had to be true.

Cold air brushed down Ben's neck. A voice began to hiss, words too low to hear.

Ben jumped to his feet and backed into the cavernous room. Another sound came from behind—rattling chains! He spun and came face to face with King Henry VIII in his massive suit of armor. Henry VIII had executed two wives and many friends. What would his ghost do?

Ben froze, not knowing where to run.

A gigantic shadow moved across the far wall. What was that?

Henry VIII's massive suit of armor creaked. Zooks! The King raised his deadly, ten-foot-long lance. He began moving slowly across the floor—aiming straight at him.

"No!" Ben shouted. "Leave me alone!" Then he added, "Please, Your Great Majesty, go away."

An arm grabbed hold of him, crushing his chest, yet when he looked down, there was nothing there! He gasped as the chilling cold turned his breath to mist.

Lashing out, Ben's shoulder connected with the King's lance. The lance crashed down. Then down went

King Henry's suit of armor—
codpiece and all.

Bang, bang, crash!

The Armories door burst
open, and two warders
charged in.

Ben rolled under the
nearest wooden horse.

A hand grabbed his tunic
and hauled him out.

"What are you doing here?"
a warder shouted, his big nos-
trils flaring.

"He's just a kid," said the other warder, a man with a
round, pink face. "Look at him."

"A kid who's up to no good. What are you doing
here?" the first warder yelled.

Ben felt like wailing. At least he'd never seen these
two nightshift guards before; they didn't realize he was a
prisoner. He had to pull himself together and not give it
away. He tried to look like some stupid, innocent kid.

"Cat got your tongue, boy?" the first warder said.

Ben said nothing.

The pink-faced warder shook his head. "He seems a
bit of a ninny. Maybe something's wrong with him. What
should we do with him?"

"Stick him in the Cradle Tower," the first warder
replied. "A Beefeater will deal with him in the morning."

CHAPTER TWELVE

THE TOWER OF LONDON

A shove from behind sent Ben sprawling into a cell.
The heavy wooden door slammed.

He was a prisoner all over again! It was all for nothing.

He lay on the cold floor, fuming mad and trussed up like a chicken. He had to get loose. Time was running out. At any moment, they'd find the warder he'd left in the rat dungeon.

Think! Think!

He still had the dagger in his boot. Luckily the guards hadn't spotted that. It took some awkward twisting to first get the dagger out and then cut the rope.

Flush with success, he leaped to his feet.

Now to get to the roof.

He studied the cold fireplace and stepped into the hearth. The only way out was up.

Ben braced his arms and legs on both sides of the chimney flue. Smooth and sooty, it was impossible to get a grip on anything. How did the chimney sweeps' boys do this?

Wedging his knees tightly against the flue sides, he stretched his arms overhead. Then he pressed with his elbows and brought up his knees. Bit by bit, he raised himself higher. Soot itched his eyes, and stone scraped his elbows over and over.

The chimney narrowed. Uh oh. He could barely fit.

Suddenly his body jammed.

He was stuck.

Panic washed over him. No wonder chimney sweeps sent such skinny kids up these things.

Sweating, he tried to go back down again.

Zooks! Couldn't do that either. His trousers were all twisted up, jamming him in place. He tried to take them off, wiggling, stretching, and gasping so hard that he inhaled a mouthful of soot and ashes.

Choking, Ben fought for air. This horrible chimney had no draft and the damp plaster stank. Desperate, he tucked one arm tight to his side, stretched the other overhead, and shoved with his feet. Yes! He managed to move. But was he just jamming himself in further?

He shoved again.

Inch by inch, he forced himself up until his head wiggled through a small circular opening—the smoke vent. He was *nearly out!*

This would be a tight fit. But he could do it. He *had* to do it.

Panting, he wiggled his body through and fell, gasping, onto the roof.

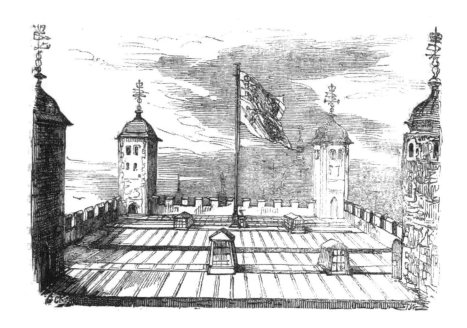

Hurrah!

Soot covered him from head to toe. He coughed, muffling the noise with his shirt. The night air smelled like freedom, but it was too soon to celebrate. If he was careless, he'd blow it.

Carefully, he inched to the roof's edge. Nearby, narrow turret windows watched like half-closed eyes. Atop the fortress's outer wall stood an armed sentry guard.

Wispy fog made the dark night darker. It rolled across the moat below. He scanned the moat's outer banks.

He longed to see Tim's skinny shape, but not a soul lay in sight.

A door in a far turret creaked open. Icy with fear, Ben crouched down. Two hefty men-at-arms strode onto the roof. They were close, scary close. And one carried a glowing torch.

Trembling, Ben's fingers closed over the dagger. Better to fight for his life than be imprisoned and executed.

"How now?" a deep voice called.

"All's well," another replied.

What a relief, just a change of guard. Quiet as a mouse, he waited until they moved away.

His foot brushed a stone that had broken from the wall. What luck—he'd need a rock.

Then he turned his eyes back to the moat.

As the clouds lifted, a sickle moon lit the riverbank. A small figure with bowlegs stood near the water. Tim! Good old Tim!

Buzzing with relief, Ben was about to wave when a tall man strode along the bank, headed straight for his friend.

CHAPTER THIRTEEN

THE TOWER OF LONDON

Ben watched with relief as the man cast a fishing line into the water. Thank God he was just a fisherman. But he was a talkative one. And now he was chatting to Tim.

After what felt like ages, the fisherman left with a couple of wiggling fish.

Ben leaned out and waved. But Tim was looking in the other direction.

Pulling off his white shirt, he waved it furiously. He prayed Tim would notice fast. If a sentry saw him, he'd be finished.

For a long while, Tim paced to and fro.

"Come on, Tim, come on," Ben muttered, waving the shirt like crazy.

Then, thank heavens, Tim waved back and sprinted

to the bank facing Cradle Tower. When he arrived, he waved again.

Ready for action, Ben wrapped the stone in the shirt and attached it to the fishing line. His arms still sore and shaking from the climb, he flung the rock as hard as he could.

It flew, the line trailing out.

Tense, Ben watched.

The stone had a long way to go—over the moat, over the high defensive wall, all the way to the bank where Tim stood waiting.

It didn't make it.

Splash!

The stone landed right in the moat.

He cringed. What if a sentry heard the splash? Flickering torches shone in every arched doorway. None moved.

Good. Try again.

He hauled the line back up and flung the stone again.

Again, it missed.

Any other day this would be easier. Tonight, he was exhausted and bruised all over. He braced his body and threw again.

This time the stone flew over the moat, over the wall, and landed on the outer bank. Yes! He felt like stomping out a victory dance.

Heart pounding, he watched Tim run forward and tie a rope to the fishing line. As fast as possible, Ben hauled it up, bringing the attached rope. Breathing hard, he secured his end of the rope to a cannon. Below, Tim tied the other end of the rope to a tree.

It now hung suspended at an angle over the moat.

Would it be strong enough to hold his weight?

If not, he'd land in the stinky moat.

Well, it was now or never. Ben straddled the rope with his back to Tim. Half sick with tension, he began to inch his way down, moving hand over hand.

So far, it was holding. He just had to keep going. Fast but steady.

Partway down, the rope sagged, and his body swung around.

Shocked, he nearly lost his hold.

He clung on, but now he was hanging under the rope. This was worse. Much worse. He clung on with his hands and legs. Don't panic, he told himself. Just keep moving.

Then something worse happened. The rope started stretching, sinking toward the moat's poopy water.

Drenched with sweat, fingers numb, he wiggled along the slackening line as best he could.

Almost there . . . almost there!

Then, to his relief, his toes touched the outer wall that ran along the riverbank. But the rope was really drooping. His head hung lower than his feet. He was nearly upside down!

The wall was right there. He simply needed to drop onto it and then jump down to Tim's side. But he couldn't move.

Sweating, straining, he gritted his teeth and tried to heave his body.

The rope swayed.

And dropped further.

This was an impossible angle. He groaned in despair. Hands grabbed hold of his ankles.

"What are you doing?" Tim whispered.

"Tim!" he stammered. "Help me!"

"Why are you hanging there?" Tim hissed.

"I'm stuck. Help, before I fall in!"

"Oh. Right." Tim pulled. "I've got you, mate."

Hands raw with rope burns, Ben slid onto the thick wall and lay gasping.

"You alright?" Tim whispered. "You look awful."

"I've been better. Oh man, I'm so glad to see you." Ben sat up and hugged his friend.

Tim hugged him back, hard. "Glad to see you, mate. But we gotta go."

Ben rubbed his aching arms. "Which way?"

Tim pointed at a torchlight flickering on the Tower Green. "A guard's coming. Hurry, follow me. I borrowed a rowboat."

"Lead on." Ben couldn't believe he was out of that cursed Tower.

With Tim's help, he climbed down the high wall and ran to the rowboat, stashed on the bank. Quickly, they each grabbed an oar.

Tim hissed, "Where to now?"

"I don't know." Ben pointed upriver. "Row till we're out of sight."

They angled the rowboat into the fast-running River Thames. Dark waves grabbed them, rocking them side to side. Ben tried to paddle, but the boat began spinning out of control.

"It's the tide!" Tim gasped. "It's rushing out and carrying us with it!"

The mighty River Thames, whipped by North Sea winds, was running wild. Not even expert boaters could navigate under London Bridge on a rushing tide.

The rowboat took off, flying through the heaving swells. Frantic, Ben tried to control it. He didn't have a chance. They were headed straight for the massive stone pilings that propped up London Bridge.

"Row!" he shouted. "Row! We're about to shoot the bridge!"

But they weren't shooting the bridge. They were about to crash. The pilings and arches loomed.

Frantically he tried to turn the boat.

He couldn't.

Smash!

They slammed side on with a horrible grinding noise. They were jammed against the pilings.

CHAPTER FOURTEEN

THE RIVER THAMES

"Hoy! Hang on there, boys!" a fisherman shouted.

Others ran out of their cottages carrying candles.

"Hang on, lads," someone yelled. "Try to push off with your oars!"

Everyone yelled advice, none of it any use. The rowboat rocked violently and tilted sideways.

"We're going to overturn!" Ben cried. "Can you swim?"

Tim's face was white as a ghost. "No."

"Me neither." Had he escaped from the Tower of London just to drown in the River Thames?

People emerged from pubs to gather on the bridge. They leaned over and shouted advice. A street vendor dropped a basket attached to a rope. As it swung overhead, Ben made a grab for it.

"Good lad!" a loud voice yelled.

"Catch it! Come on, lad, you can do it!" a woman shouted.

The basket smacked Ben's skull and swung out of reach.

A man roared with laughter. "You're going to drown, you nincompoops!"

Ben made another wild grab for the basket, nearly falling into the raging water. He flashed a look back at the Tower. Two silhouettes with flickering torches were heading fast in their direction.

"The guards are coming!" he stammered and scanned the wild waters. "We can climb onto the pilings and try to reach the shore."

"No!" Tim wailed. "We'll drown for sure."

"Zooks!" Ben yelled. "Look what's coming now!"

A massive storm surge—huge waves foaming with rubbish—bore down on them. It smashed into the boat and lifted it clear of the pilings. For a petrifying moment, it hovered atop a wave.

"Row," Ben shouted. "Row!"

With all his strength, he dug in with his oar. Beside him, Tim grunted with effort.

Like a cork, the suddenly freed rowboat shot downriver.

The crowd on the bridge cheered. Ben grinned and waved his oar. He'd always had a secret wish to shoot the bridge. Pa said the sailors who did that were crazy as loons.

Teeth clenched, they used the oars to steer as the Thames carried them on a rollicking ride.

"We've got to get out of London," Tim shouted.

"I know. I'm sorry, Tim!" The wind whipped the words from Ben's mouth.

The prow collided with a mound of oyster beds, tumbling them both into the shallows. Panting, they tugged the boat over the sharp oyster shells and up the bank. Turning the boat upside down, they crawled underneath and huddled together, shivering.

"What happened in the Tower?" Tim asked. "Why were you arrested?"

Quickly, Ben told him the whole story.

"So, Princess Elizabeth never escaped after all that?" Tim asked.

"No, she's still locked up somewhere in there. And Queen Mary wants to have her head cut off. The Princess is innocent. She told me all about it. You should have heard her, Tim."

Teeth chattering, Tim wrapped his arms around his chest. "But what can anyone do about it?"

"We could find her supporters and warn them she's being taken to trial this week," Ben said. "Maybe they could watch for the barge and board it on its way to Westminster. They could still save her. Too bad that strange Earl of Devon was arrested. He would have helped her."

"He's been freed," Tim said. "I saw him riding out of London in his carriage. I reckon he'll be heading to his castle in the countryside."

"What? How?"

"I don't know."

Ben shivered. "I must tell him about the Westminster

plans. If he can get her off the barge and on her way to France, she'll be safe from Queen Mary."

"Maybe," Tim said, his teeth chattering. "Let's get out from under here. I'm freezing."

Ben nodded. "Maybe we'll warm up if we start walking."

Dripping with water and mud, they made their way along the road.

A plump woman emerged from behind a hedge. "You two young rascals look wet and hungry. Would you like to warm up and have a bite to eat?"

Ben shot Tim a questioning look, and Tim nodded.

Ben smiled. "Thank you, ma'am, that sounds good."

The woman led them along a path, stopping near a small cottage.

"Wait here a minute." She went and knocked at the door.

A hefty-looking man in dark trousers and a white undervest appeared. The woman spoke to him and then beckoned to the boys.

Ben's stomach rumbled. He ran up with Tim close behind. The woman bid them goodnight and walked away.

Ben waved at her. "Thank you!"

He turned to greet the cottage owner, and his eyes widened.

To his horror, the man was buttoning a policeman's blue jacket.

"Run!" he yelled, grabbing Tim's arm. "Run!"

CHAPTER FIFTEEN

THE RIVER THAMES

Ben and Tim ran until the shadows swallowed them up. When they could run no longer, they crawled beneath a thick hedge and hunkered down. At least it was dry and somewhat warm. Gratefully, Ben sank into a deep sleep.

He woke to the feel of hot sun filtering through the thick foliage.

"What now?" Tim asked. "We can't go back to London."

Ben nodded, truly sorry that he'd ruined things for Tim. "We keep on our way to the Earl's castle. We'll tell him what we know. Maybe he and his friends can save the Princess. And maybe he'll take pity on us and toss us another coin."

"It's the best plan we've got," Tim said.

Together, the friends set out. Two days later, they

stood side by side and stared up at the Earl's gleaming turrets.

"Very grand," Ben said. "But how will we get inside to talk to the Earl? The place is locked up like a vault. High walls, moat, even a drawbridge. They'll never let us past the gatehouse. Look at us!" He sniffed his muddy shirt. It stank.

"Someone's coming," Tim said.

Galloping hooves thundered down the road toward them. A group of riders appeared. What a relief; leading the group was the Earl of Devon. He wore an elaborate leather hunting costume with lace ruffles at his neck and a purple feather in his hat.

Spotting Ben and Tim, he frowned. Then recognition dawned, for his eyes widened.

Ben ran into the road. "Sir! Sir Edward!"

The Earl waved at his companions to ride on. Perched on his prancing horse, he stared down at Ben. "You c-c-called out to me, lad?"

"Yes, sir." Ben lowered his voice. "I delivered your orange with the message to Princess Elizabeth, sir. But the rescue attempt failed. Princess Elizabeth is still in the Tower, and soon she'll be on trial in Westminster. She could be executed, sir. I've come to tell you, as I know you'll want to help."

The Earl's face turned red. He glanced at the gatehouse where his companions stood, watching with interest. "I gave you no message for Princess Elizabeth," he said. "I've never seen you before in my life."

"But you did, sir." Ben flushed with confusion. "You

came to my coal cart in London and asked me to take her oranges. I helped her see the invisible message, sir."

If he hoped the Earl might have a word of praise or a coin, he was mistaken. The Earl's lips were pressed tightly together.

Why was the Earl acting so strange?

An elegant older lady in a blue riding suit and a silver-plumed hat broke away from the party at the gates. She approached on horseback. "What is going on, Edward?"

The Earl flashed her an annoyed glance. "Nothing mother. Everything is fine."

Ben tried again, this time raising his voice.

"Queen Mary won't allow Princess Elizabeth any visitors, sir. Your rescue attempt failed, and the Princess is in danger. They're taking her by barge to Winchester to be tried this week. Queen Mary could execute her."

The Earl's face turned purple. "I d-d-don't know who you are or what you're talking about."

The Earl's mother shot Ben a worried glance. Was it possible she was a friend of the Princess?

"Sir, please," Ben said. "You can't let her die! You know she is innocent. She is not a traitor. You have to stop the Queen."

"How dare you talk treason against Queen Mary?" he demanded.

"But you—"

The Earl drew back in his saddle, and his horse reared. Ben dodged clear of the thrashing hooves. Two hunting dogs, big greyhounds, snarled and bared their pointed teeth.

The Earl said, "Queen Mary is my b-b-beloved second c-cousin."

"Beloved! But she had you arrested last week!"

"Enough," he snarled. "We are to b-b-be married."

"Married! You and the Queen?" Ben gasped.

To his surprise, behind the Earl's back, the elegant woman grimaced.

"Yes," the Earl said. "And we w-w-will rule England together." He pulled himself straight in the saddle and glowered down at Ben. "So, t-t-tell me, boy, are you talking about treason?"

"But you gave me a message for the Princess. And you paid me, sir."

"Yes, look." Tim fumbled in his pocket for the money Ben had shared with him after they'd bought the pies.

"This here's the change."

The Earl's eyes narrowed. "So, you are a t-t-thief as well as a liar! Where did you steal those from? The constable will put you in the stocks and flog you. That's what we do here with t-t-thieves, vagrants, and liars." Waving at his gatehouse, he shouted, "Guards! Guards! Seize these good-for-nothing thieves."

The Earl's mother bit her lip, her cheeks turning crimson. Her white horse tossed its silky mane.

"Princess Elizabeth is your cousin, too!" Ben cried. "Once you wanted to marry *her* and rule England at her side. Now it seems you're not so honor-bound to protect her!" Then he grabbed Tim's arm. "Run!"

With hunting dogs barking and guards shouting, Ben and Tim scrambled over a thicket and sprinted into the dense woods.

When they were safe, they flopped down in a grassy clearing.

Tim spoke first. "The Earl called us treasonous? He's

the treasonous one. First, he sided with the Princess and then with the Queen. He'll sell himself for power."

Ben nodded, thinking hard. "But that grand-looking lady, did you see her face? She might be the Earl's mother, but I think she's also Princess Elizabeth's friend."

"I saw it, too. She looked worried."

Ben put his head in his hands. "We've done all we can. We must pray that lady will carry our warning to someone who can help."

CHAPTER SIXTEEN

OXFORDSHIRE
SIX WEEKS LATER

Sunshine shimmered on the slowly flowing River Thames. White swans floated by. A tern dove into the water with a splash and popped back up with a silver fish in its beak.

"We've caught two fat salmon," Ben said. "We can sell them for a few farthings at the Sonning market. Let's go there now. There'll be a newsboy—he'll know if there's any news about Princess Elizabeth."

"Good idea. And the market has music on Saturday," Tim said. "Maybe the juggler will be there."

"Right, let's go," Ben said.

They scampered down the country road, hurrying past green fields dotted with white cottages.

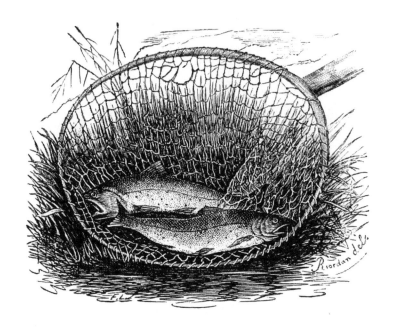

Ben doubted he'd be recognized as an escaped prisoner, for the village of Sonning was a long way from London. Just in case, though, he always wore a wide-brimmed hat when he went to market.

As they neared the small hamlet, he pulled his hat brim down low. Church bells started ringing, clanging in the bright air.

Crowds, much larger than usual, filled the streets.

"Whoa, big market today," Ben said.

"They're not here for the market," said a pink-cheeked woman. "A royal procession's coming our way."

Oh no, Bloody Mary was coming? With her guards? Would he be recognized?

Ben gulped. "The Queen is coming?"

"Not the Queen."

"Then who?"

The woman beamed. "Princess Elizabeth!"

"She's alive?" Ben blurted. "She escaped the Tower? They didn't cut off her head?"

"No, indeed, they did not." She tapped her nose. "Rumor has it a friend changed the Queen's mind."

A thrill ran through Ben. Could the friend be the Earl's mother, the elegant lady on the white horse? "So she's free?"

The woman laughed. "Dear me, no. She's still Bloody Mary's prisoner, but she's to live in Woodstock Castle. She'll be much happier there. Now hold your tongue and watch the road! Here they come. I've got to try to see her. I love the Princess." The woman ran forward, carrying a posy of violets.

Tim grabbed Ben's arm. "Careful, she's still under guard. Stay out of sight!"

"They won't notice me," Ben said.

Tim tried to pull him back. "What are you doing? There must be more than a hundred troops!"

"I want to see her. Just for a minute." Ben pulled his hat lower.

Tim groaned.

Troops, dressed in blue livery, surrounded the royal, white-curtained litter. Excited, cheering people ran up, piling sweetmeats and nosegays onto the conveyance.

A baker shouted, "God save you, Princess!"

Ben's heart swelled with joy and relief when Princess Elizabeth's small, pointed face peered out from the curtain. She looked healthy and even a little happy.

She waved at the crowd and her voice rang out. "Good people, save these wondrous cakes for your own enjoyment."

Turning, she caught sight of Ben. Her dark eyes widened as he raised his chin and their eyes met.

For a long moment, their gazes locked.

A small grin quirked the corner of her mouth and she gave him the briefest nod.

Ben shot her a half-smile and plucked at his hat brim.

Clearly, they both knew the danger he was in, for she quickly turned to a group of cheering children.

He remembered that frantic moment switching clothes with her and cracked a grin. By St. George, he was glad they were out of the Tower.

"Let's go," Ben told Tim.

"About time," Tim said.

But before leaving, he turned one last time to see Princess Elizabeth flashing him a grateful, knowing smile. And then the litter moved on and she was lost from sight.

Leaving the crowds, the boys bought apple pies and sat behind a hedge to picnic.

"That was a bit close for comfort," Tim said.

Ben said. "We're wanted men. We can never go back to London."

Tim took a big bite of pie. "No problem. I like living in the country. And fishing for a living is good."

Ben laughed. "It sure beats hauling coal. Maybe someday we can buy a small fishing boat—when Princess Elizabeth is Queen. Because then we'll be safe to do what we want. We'll finally be free."

CHAPTER SEVENTEEN

Over the next four years, Ben often thought of his friend, the Princess. Elizabeth was still a prisoner in Woodstock Castle; it was much nicer than the Tower of London, but she could never leave.

Then one day, he heard that their mutual enemy, Queen Mary, had died.

On a frosty morning in January 1559, Princess Elizabeth was crowned Queen of England.

In mid-June, Ben was surprised to receive a royal summons to Windsor Castle.

In the Gothic Chapel of the Order of the Garter, tall stained-glass windows cast flashes of blue, green, and red colors on Elizabeth's white dress. Sparkles shone in her diamond coronet.

Ben knelt before the newly crowned Queen Elizabeth, and she greeted him with dark, solemn eyes.

Her voice rang out. "Ben Forrester, you have been a brave, trustworthy, and faithful friend, despite torture and at the risk of your own life."

Ben bowed his head, humbled yet proud.

She spoke again with a smile in her voice. "And now, it is my pleasure to confer knighthood on to you."

Knighthood!

Ben gasped. With his head still bowed, he felt the Queen tap him with the flat surface of a knighting sword —first on his right shoulder and then on his left.

"Be thou a knight in the name of God," she said. "Rise up, Sir Ben."

Sir Ben. He was a knight!

Hardly believing what was happening, he rose to his feet.

Her face solemn, her eyes sparkling with gratitude, Queen Elizabeth presented him with the insignia of his new order, riding spurs, and a sword.

Ben recited the age-old Knights' Code of Chivalry:

I promise on my faith to fear God and maintain His Church, to serve the Queen, to protect the weak and defenseless, to live by honor, to fight for the welfare of all, to obey those placed in authority, to guard the honor of fellow knights, to eschew unfairness, meanness and deceit, to speak the truth, to respect the honor of women, to never refuse a challenge from an equal, and to never turn my back upon a foe.

The new Queen gave Ben a beautiful chestnut horse and Tim a glossy black one. The boys rode back to Sonning and arrived at the manor house gifted to them by Elizabeth.

Ben rubbed his eyes and stared at the sprawling mansion. It lay on the banks of the sweetly flowing Thames.

"Zounds!" It was all he could think of saying.

The manor and rolling farmlands lay only a few miles from Windsor Castle. In the distance, the grand castle's turrets glowed pale pink. Like all the Queen's knights, he would be close if she needed protection.

Tim grabbed his arm and pointed. "Look!"

A flag bearing Ben's family crest flew over the manor. Ben had been proud to learn that some of his ancestors had been knights long ago.

The crest read *The Ancient Arms of Forrester*, and their family motto was *Military Fortitude and Magnanimity*.

Magnanimity meant you had a big heart and were generous. Ben liked that a lot. He hoped his parents could somehow see the crest. They'd love it.

"Zooks!" Tim said. "Who could have guessed we'd end up here!"

Ben shook his head. "I never thought I'd survive that rat dungeon or that the Princess would live. Now, she's Queen of England, I'm a knight, and you're a squire."

"It's like a dream," Tim said quietly.

"I was so glad to see you on the River Thames bank that night. Without you, I'd still be locked up. Or worse." Ben glanced at his friend. "I was scared you might have forgotten about the invisible ink and that you wouldn't find my message."

Tim shot him an embarrassed grin. "Actually, I ate the

orange and crumpled up the paper. I was about to throw it away when I remembered!"

"Good thing!"

They both laughed.

Ben breathed in the sweet-smelling air and whooped.

Spurring their horses on toward their new home, Ben shouted, "We did it. You and me. We're free. And I escaped the Tower of London!"

THE TOWER OF LONDON: 10 FASCINATING FACTS

1. William the Conqueror built it in 1066 as a castle and fortress. It became a prison in 1100.
2. Over 23,500 jewels are stored in the Tower, valued at over $32 billion.
3. 6 ravens are kept inside for superstitious reasons.
4. It once held a Royal Zoo with lions, kangaroos, polar bears, elephants, ostriches, and more.
5. 22 executions took place there. The last was a German spy who was caught parachuting into England in 1941 (WWII).
6. The Tower was besieged several times by invaders.
7. It has been a treasury, a public records office, an armory, the Royal Mint, the home of the monarchs' crown jewels, a royal living quarters, a prison, and a place of execution.
8. They say Queen Anne Boleyn's ghost walks the halls carrying her head under her arm.
9. Beefeaters and guards have reported a creepy crushing sensation in the Armory
10. The Tower of London is a World Heritage site. It's one of the most popular tourist attractions in England.

Queen Elizabeth I

Queen Elizabeth I Coat of Arms

Princess Elizabeth was born on September 7, 1533. Her father was King Henry VIII. Her mother was the King's second wife, Queen Anne Boleyn.

Elizabeth's Parents

King Henry VIII wanted a son to inherit his crown. When his first wife gave him a daughter, he ended the marriage and took a second wife: Anne Boleyn.

Unfortunately, Anne Boleyn did not produce a son. She also gave him a daughter— Elizabeth. Two and a half years later, the King had his second wife's head cut off.

The King's daughters, Mary and Elizabeth, were half-sisters but lived separately. They had little chance to get to know one another.

Finally, the King got his wish: his third wife gave him a son. The boy's health was poor, though, and he was often sick.

Princess Elizabeth was 13 when Henry VIII died. Her sickly brother became King Edward.

Elizabeth's father left her well provided for. She was an intelligent child with good tutors. She studied hard and learned many languages.

Sickly King Edward died young, and Elizabeth's big sister, Princess Mary, became queen. Unfortunately, the half-sisters did not get along. Mary was afraid that Elizabeth would steal her throne.

IMPRISONED BY HER OLDER SISTER

Queen Mary was a devout Roman Catholic. She feared that Princess Elizabeth's supporters, mostly devout Protestants, would try to overthrow her. Mary's fears were justified. They mounted an attack but failed to take Mary's throne. Furious, Mary imprisoned her sister in the Tower of London.

Elizabeth claimed she knew nothing about the Wyatt Rebellion. Mary couldn't prove that her sister was guilty. She released Elizabeth from the tower but placed her under house arrest.

Elizabeth lived as a prisoner at Woodstock Castle.

THE ELIZABETHAN AGE

When Queen Mary died, the twenty-five-year-old Princess Elizabeth was crowned Queen of England on January 15, 1558.

Queen Elizabeth refused to marry, although she had many suitors. She was determined to rule alone.

Her reign was a period of exploration and advances in the arts and technology. Sir Francis Drake and Sir Walter Raleigh explored and colonized the Americas. William Shakespeare wrote some of the most brilliant works of English literature.

With her Religious Settlement of 1559, Queen Elizabeth also helped to create the modern Church of England.

Her troops and ships defeated the Spanish Armada in 1588. After this crushing defeat of Spain, she was named 'Gloriana'. Other names were 'Good Queen Bess' and 'The Virgin Queen.'

She survived the smallpox pandemic, but the dreadful disease damaged her skin. She covered her scars with white powder.

Elizabeth dressed in elaborate, ruffled, embroidered, jewel-encrusted gowns and had many portraits painted of herself.

England's enemies tried to have her assassinated. To know who was plotting against her, she set up a spy network throughout England.

Queen Elizabeth reigned for forty-five years. England became prosperous. The Elizabethan Age is considered by many to be the golden age in the history of England.

Queen Mary I

Queen Mary I Coat of Arms

Princess Mary was King Henry VIII's first daughter. Her mother was his first wife, Queen Katherine of Aragon.

Mary was 37 when her 15-year-old half-brother, Edward, became king. Edward soon got sick, though. He decided to pass on his throne to his cousin Jane—instead of his big sister, Mary.

QUEEN JANE EXECUTED

Lady Jane Grey was queen for only nine days. Mary stepped in, along with her supporters, and had her cousin, Jane, executed. Then, Mary claimed the throne for herself.

A RELIGIOUS MASSACRE

Queen Mary married Philip II of Spain. She was extremely religious and followed the Roman Catholic faith. However, many people in England were Protestants.

Mary hated this and wanted everyone to follow her faith. She had almost 300 Protestants leaders burned at the stake when they refused to become Roman Catholic. Because of this, people called her Bloody Mary.

Imprisoned Her Sister

Mary was terrified that her half-sister, Princess Elizabeth, would try to steal her throne. Mary imprisoned Elizabeth in the Tower for two months and then put her under house arrest.

5 Year Reign

Queen Mary had no children. She ruled for five years and died at age 42 during a flu epidemic. After her death, Princess Elizabeth was named Queen of England.

Sir Edward Courtenay, the Earl of Devon

Sir Edward Courtenay Coat of Arms

Like Queen Mary, King Henry VIII feared that people wanted to steal his throne.

He was especially afraid of Sir Edward Courtney's father, a member of the House of York and considered a threat to the ruling House of Tudor.

When Sir Edward was 12, his father was executed. The boy was then locked in the Tower of London and kept prisoner for 15 years.

When Sir Edward Courtney was freed, he joined forces with Sir Thomas Wyatt. Together, they planned the Wyatt Rebellion. Edward's plan was to marry Princess Elizabeth, his second cousin, and together they could claim the throne. The plan failed and he was thrown back into the Tower.

Edward came up with a new plan: he proposed marriage to Queen Mary, who was also his second cousin.

Despite his rebellion, Queen Mary was fond of the Earl of Devon. She didn't marry him, but she allowed him to leave England and live in Europe.

A SUCCESSFUL ESCAPE FROM
THE TOWER OF LONDON

More than 8,000 unfortunate people have been imprisoned in the Tower. Some who left did so without their heads. A small number, however, managed to escape.

I Escaped books are based on exciting real-life heroes and events. The torture and escape of our hero, Ben, are based on the experiences of John Gerard in 1597.

John Gerard, a priest, was imprisoned in the Tower on charges of plotting the overthrow of Queen Elizabeth I. He was tortured, manacled, and repeatedly suspended from chains in the Torture Chamber. The torturers wanted him to reveal the whereabouts of his friends, but he refused to do so.

John Gerard came up with an escape plan and sent a message with details to his friends. He wrote in orange juice--invisible ink. John had noticed that the Cradle Tower was close to the outer wall and overlooked the moat. He decided that, with help from the outside, it might be possible to fling a rope from the Tower roof to the other side of the moat and escape.

Luckily his friends knew about invisible writing. They read his message and understood the plan. John's friends rowed a boat along the River Thames to the wall near the Cradle Tower and watched for John.

John Gerard managed, with difficulty, to reach the roof under cover of darkness. He threw down a weighted string, pulled up a rope, and climbed down the rope across the moat until he reached the outer wall. Despite nearly drowning in the River Thames high tide, he and his friends escaped.

John Gerard was nearly caught again but managed to avoid the guards searching for him. He traveled far from London and hid in the countryside. John went on to have many adventures and close escapes. His book, *The Autobiography of a Hunted Priest*, tells his amazing story.

Further studies

Download Link:
**I Escaped The Tower of London
Study Guide**

https://scottpetersbooks.com/downloads/worksheets

MAKE YOUR OWN INVISIBLE INK

Make secret messages of your own by mixing up a batch of 'invisible ink'.

INSTRUCTIONS:

1. Squeeze the juice of half an orange into a bowl
2. Add a few drops of water.
3. Mix with a spoon.
4. Dip a cotton bud (Q-tip) into the mixture and use this to write your message on a piece of white paper.
5. Wait for the message to completely dry. It will become invisible.

REVEAL YOUR MESSAGE:

Heat the paper using a light bulb and read your message.

THE I ESCAPED SERIES

I Escaped North Korea!

I Escaped The California Camp Fire

I Escaped The World's Deadliest Shark Attack

I Escaped Amazon River Pirates

I Escaped The Donner Party

I Escaped The Salem Witch Trials

I Escaped Pirates In The Caribbean

I Escaped The Tower of London

Also by Ellie Crowe

Surfer of the Century, The Life of Duke Kahanamoku

Nelson Mandela, The Boy Called Troublemaker

Also by Scott Peters

Mystery of the Egyptian Scroll

Mystery of the Egyptian Mummy

Join the I Escaped Club

Get a free pack of mazes and word finds to print and play!

https://www.subscribepage.com/escapedclub

BIBLIOGRAPHY

Abbott, Geoff, *Ghosts of the Tower of London,* A David & Charles Book © F&W Media International

Ainsworth, William, *The Tower of London, a Historical Romance,* A. L. Burt, New York

Elson, George, *The Last of the Climbing Boys,* Victorian London eBooks, 1900.

Gerard, John, *The Autobiography of a Hunted Priest,* Ignatius Press

Ducksters: https://www.ducksters.com/history/ middle_ages/becoming_a_medieval_knight

IMAGES

The Tower of London Map - Thomas Römer, CC BY-SA 3.0

Ben in the dungeon - Sue Wyshynski

Princess Elizabeth - Sue Wyshynski

Traitors' Gate, Old London Bridge - Robert Chambers

Tower stairs door - George Cruikshank

Swimming rats - V. H. Darwin

Tower drawbridge - George Cruikshank

Tower roof summit - George Cruikshank

Knight ceremony - Henry Marriot Paget

Manor house - Frederick Bligh Bond

Made in the USA
Las Vegas, NV
15 December 2024

13808782R00072